This Ladybird retelling
by
Nicola Baxter

Published by Ladybird Books Ltd
80 Strand London WC2R 0RL
A Penguin Company
20
© LADYBIRD BOOKS LTD 1993

Printed in Italy

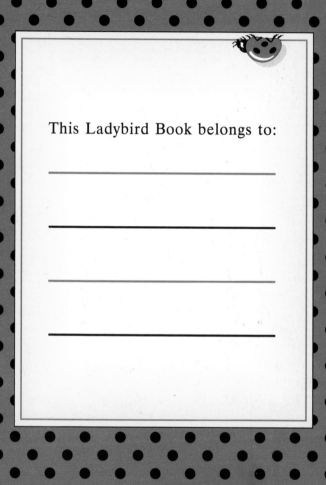

This Ladybird Book belongs to:

_____

_____

_____

_____

FAVOURITE TALES

Rapunzel

*illustrated
by
MARTIN AITCHISON*

based on the story by Jacob and Wilhelm Grimm

Once upon a time, in a faraway land, there lived a man and his wife. They had a pretty little house and all that they needed, but one thing made them unhappy.

"If only we had a child of our own to love and look after," they sighed.

Next to their house stood an old
mansion with a beautiful garden.
People said that a wicked witch lived
there. One day, the wife glimpsed
some lettuces growing in the
next-door garden.

Although she went on with her work, the lettuces stayed in her mind. Finally, she said to her husband, "I feel I shall die if I don't taste one of those crisp, green lettuces. Won't you please climb over the wall and get one for me?"

Her husband was afraid to go into the garden, so at first he refused. But as the days passed, the wife's yearning for the lettuces grew, until at last she became quite ill.

One night, the man could bear it no longer, and he climbed over the wall. As his feet touched the ground, he nearly fainted with fright. There before him stood the witch.

"How dare you come creeping into my garden?" she snarled.

"I must have some lettuces for my wife," the man pleaded. "She is ill, and she will die without them."

"Take the lettuces, then," said the witch. "But in return, you must give your firstborn child to me."

The man was so terrified that he agreed. Grabbing a handful of lettuces, he fled back to his wife.

Some time later, a beautiful baby girl was born to the man and his wife. That same day, the witch appeared at their door. Reminding the man of his promise, she took the baby away.

The witch named the child Rapunzel,
and she looked after her well. Every
year the girl grew more lovely.

So that no one should ever see how beautiful she was, the witch shut Rapunzel up in a high tower in the forest. The tower had no door and no staircase – just one window right at the top.

Only the witch ever visited poor Rapunzel. She would call out,

"Rapunzel, Rapunzel,
Let down your hair."

Rapunzel's hair shone like gold in the sun, and it was so long that it reached from the top of the tower right down to the ground.

Huffing and puffing, the wicked witch would slowly climb the tower, holding on to Rapunzel's lovely hair. Then she would climb in through the window.

Years passed, and Rapunzel never set
eyes on another living person. Then,
one day, a young prince riding
through the forest heard Rapunzel's
sweet singing.

"I have never heard such a lovely voice," he said to himself. "I shall not rest until I find out who it belongs to."

So the Prince hid nearby and saw the witch climb the tower.

That evening, after the witch had gone, the Prince called out,

*"Rapunzel, Rapunzel,
Let down your hair."*

Rapunzel was astonished to see a young man climb through the window. And the Prince was dazzled by the lovely girl. As they spoke to each other, they realised they were in love.

"I will come back tomorrow night to rescue you," the Prince promised.

When the witch returned the next day, she saw at once that Rapunzel's heart was full of love for a stranger.

"You have betrayed me, you wicked girl!" she shrieked furiously. With her sharp scissors, she went *snipper snap!* and cut off Rapunzel's hair. Then she took the girl to a distant desert and left her there, alone and weeping.

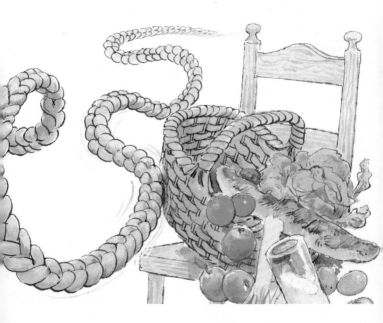

The witch returned to the tower to
wait for the Prince. At last she heard
him call,

> *"Rapunzel, Rapunzel,*
> *Let down your hair,"*

and she lowered the golden plait for
him to climb.

When the Prince found himself face to face with the angry witch, he leapt in despair from the tower. He fell into a thicket of briars, which scratched his eyes and blinded him.

For years the Prince wandered
through many lands, until one day,
in a lonely desert, he heard the lovely
voice that he had never forgotten.

"Rapunzel!" he cried, throwing his arms around her. Rapunzel's tears of joy fell on the Prince's eyes and healed them. Once more he saw her beautiful face.

The Prince took Rapunzel's hand and
led her to his kingdom, where they
were married with great rejoicing.

And there, safe at last from the wicked witch, Rapunzel and her Prince lived happily ever after.